D1717938

tail tale

ANUSHKA RAVISHANKAR · TUSHAR VAYEDA · MAYUR VAYEDA

Cat is fed up with her tail
It never does what it should
It waves, it twitches and it flicks
It's always up to its own tricks
And does no real good

Cat now wants a brand new tail
A tail that she can choose
Something clever, something bold
A tail that does just what it's told
And has a proper use

Dog wags his tail
Madly when he's merry
Cat thinks that is rather
Extraordinary

So Cat waylays Dog
Who yelps, with a whine,
That's not my tail, it's a —

long straight

line

Mouse has a tail
That helps him lose heat
Aha, thinks Cat,
That's such a cool feat

So Cat swipes at Mouse
Who squeaks, What a tangle!
That's not my tail, it's a —

big
rOund
bangle

Pig's tail is cute
It coils like a spring
Thinks Cat, it might be
A jolly sort of thing

Cat bounds to Pig
Who squeals, with a giggle,
That's not my tail, it's a—

curly shaped
squiggle

The long tail of Snake
Lets him slither around
Might be fun, muses Cat,
To crawl on the ground

Cat seeks out Snake
Who sneers, What a mess!
That's not a tail,
It's the alphabet—

ssssssssss

'Then Cat suddenly sees a tail
The best she ever saw
It's silky, soft and glossy too
It's moving fast... But with a mew,
Cat grabs it with her paw—

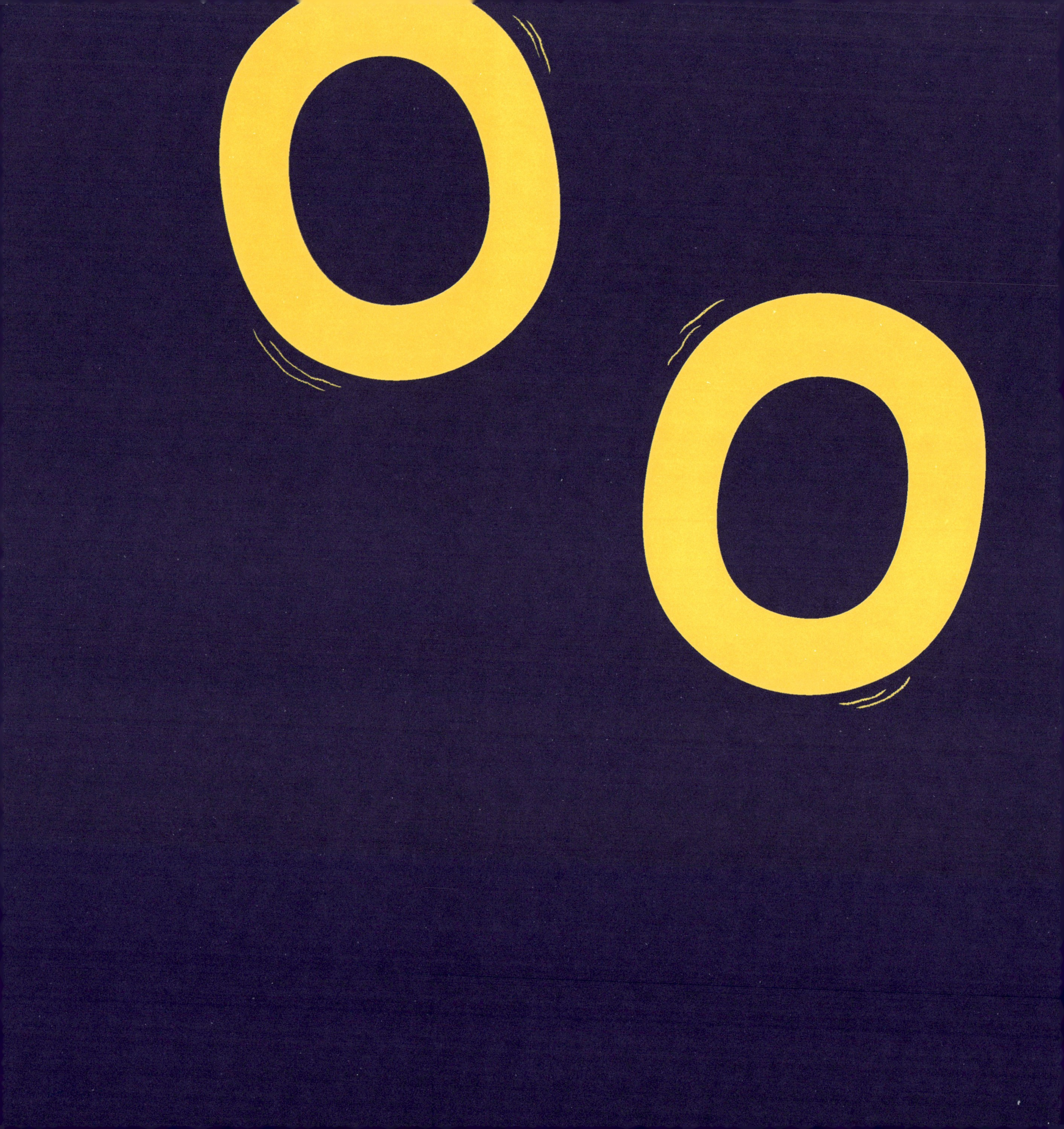
O
O

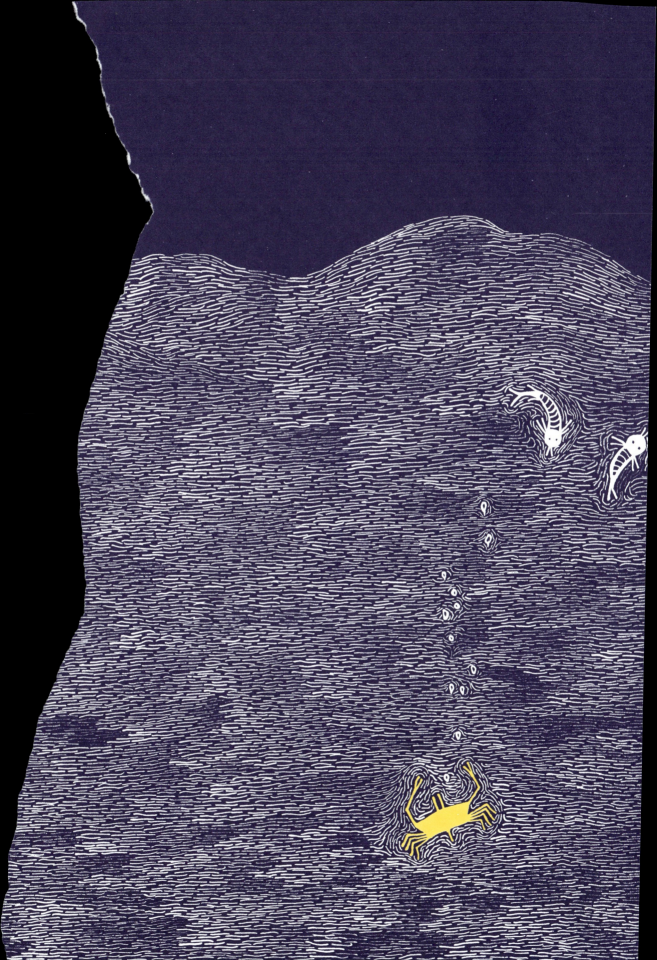

So Cat decides to keep
It's cleverer than she
It waves in warning when
It stands up straight when s
It lands her on her feet w

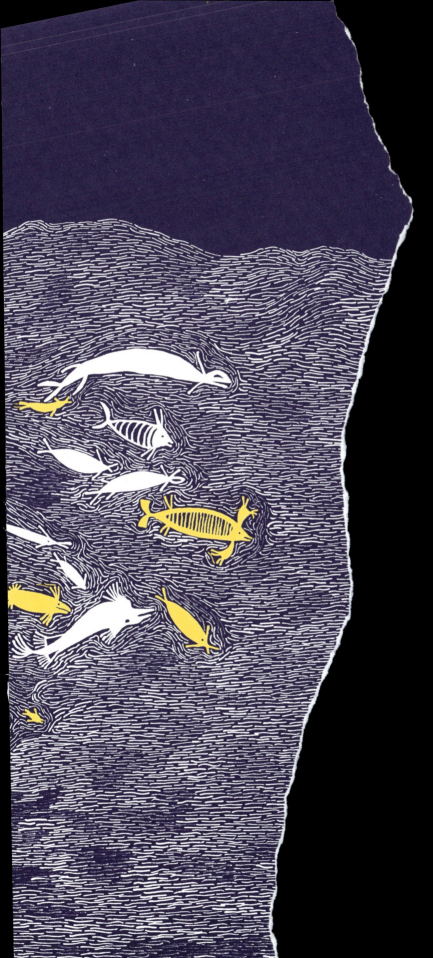

p her tail
thought —
she's teased
he is pleased
ith ease

And it's all she's got.

THE BROTHERS TUSHAR AND MAYUR VAYEDA come from the Warli village of Ganjad in Maharashtra. After their schooling – their grandfather started the first school in the village – they went on to college in Mumbai, studying animation and business management.

It was only during the early years of their college life that they started paying more attention to the traditional art that had always surrounded them in their native village. They realized just how special it was. They also became convinced that their roots were in the village, with the Warli indigenous community.

The brothers enjoyed working with each other, and decided to hone up on their Warli art skills – the basics of which they had picked up as youngsters. As their mastery over the form grew, they became keen to do something else: to try and render new experiences while keeping to the basics of their inherited style.

Even though they had decided to live and work in Ganjad, they knew the importance of travel, and were aware of how it had expanded their world view. This understanding forms the basis of their artistic and cultural vision: to stretch the boundaries of Warli art, without losing its essence. They see this as their way of contributing to the growth of the community.

ANUSHKA RAVISHANKAR is considered the finest English language children's poet in India. She started her career as a programmer and systems analyst before she switched from writing computer programs to writing absurd verse for children.

Anushka worked as an editor with Tara Books from 1996 to 2001. Her first book published by Tara was *Tiger on a Tree*— a picture book with absurd verse, which went on to become a children's classic. The first edition came out in 1997, and it has been in print ever since. Over the years, Anushka has written over thirty-five books for children, including picture books in verse, chapter books, retellings of folk tales and non-fiction. However, absurd verse has remained her favourite genre. Several of her books have been published internationally and have won awards, including the South Asia Book Award, the Andersen Award and several Special Mentions in the International White Ravens Catalogue.

She has conducted readings and workshops for children in France, Germany, UK, USA and India. Some of her books for Tara include *Captain Coconut and the Case of the Missing Bananas, Tiger on a Tree, Catch That Crocodile!, To Market! To Market!, Alphabets are Amazing Animals* and *Hic!*

Tail Tale is her twentieth book for Tara.

TAIL TALE
Copyright © 2019 Tara Books Pvt. Ltd.
For the text: Anushka Ravishankar
For the illustrations: Tushar Vayeda and Mayur Vayeda

Tara Books Pvt. Ltd., India < www.tarabooks.com >
and
Tara Publishing Ltd., UK < www.tarabooks.com/uk >

Design: Dhwani Shah

Production: C. Arumugam

Printed in India by
Canara Traders and Printers Pvt. Ltd.

Cover screen-printed and bound at
AMM Screens, Chennai, India.

ISBN: 978-81-934485-7-1

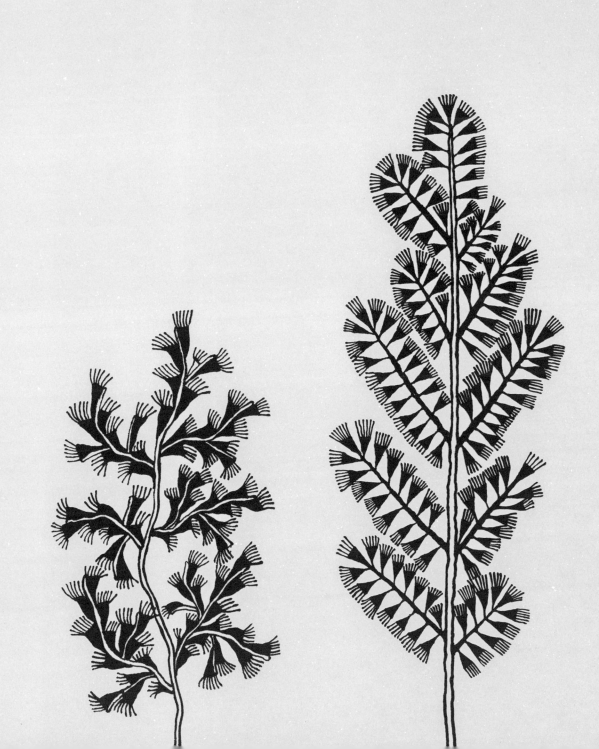